To..
....
....

This book invites you
to a Halloween Scare

Prepare If You Dare

A Halloween Scare in GEORGIA

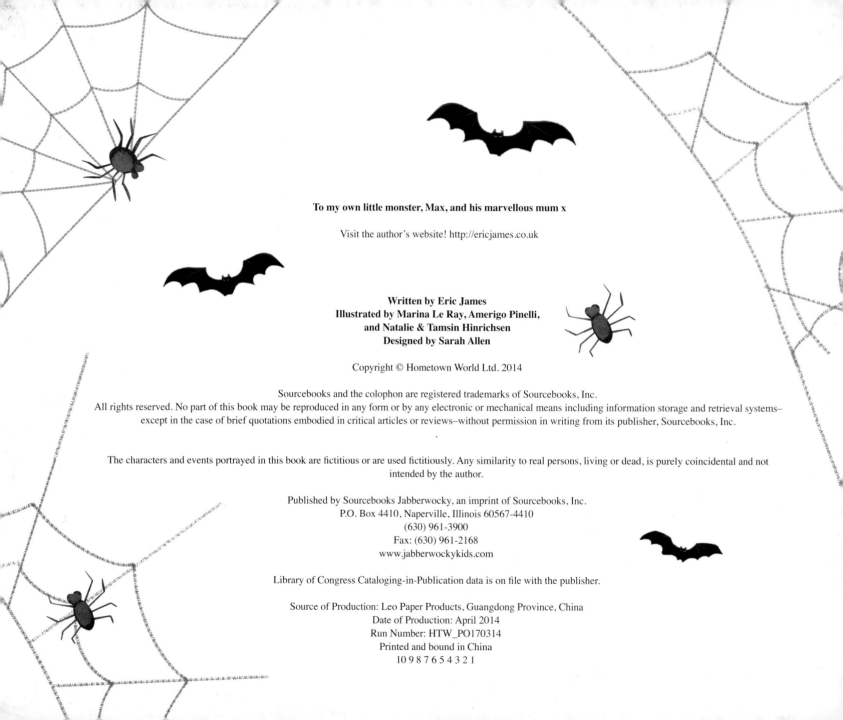

To my own little monster, Max, and his marvellous mum x

Visit the author's website! http://ericjames.co.uk

Written by Eric James
Illustrated by Marina Le Ray, Amerigo Pinelli,
and Natalie & Tamsin Hinrichsen
Designed by Sarah Allen

Copyright © Hometown World Ltd. 2014

Published by Sourcebooks Jabberwocky, an imprint of Sourcebooks, Inc.
P.O. Box 4410, Naperville, Illinois 60567-4410
(630) 961-3900
Fax: (630) 961-2168
www.jabberwockykids.com

Library of Congress Cataloging-in-Publication data is on file with the publisher.

Source of Production: Leo Paper Products, Guangdong Province, China
Date of Production: April 2014
Run Number: HTW_PO170314
Printed and bound in China
10 9 8 7 6 5 4 3 2 1

Prepare If You Dare

A Halloween Scare in GEORGIA

Written by Eric James

Illustrated by Marina Le Ray

sourcebooks
jabberwocky

A tale full of sights that are best left unseen.
You ready? You sure?
This was my Halloween.

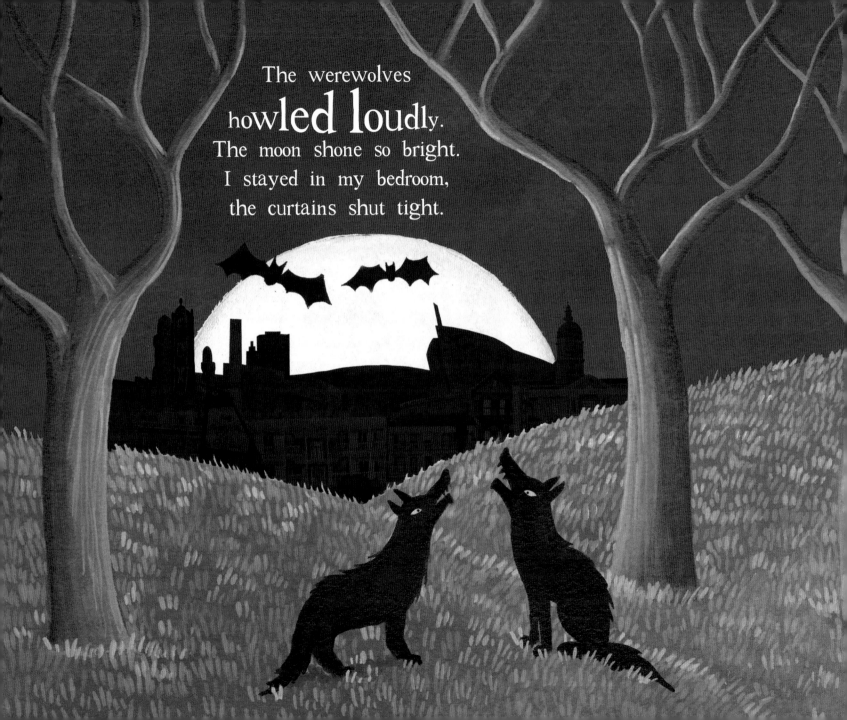

The werewolves howled loudly.
The moon shone so bright.
I stayed in my bedroom,
the curtains shut tight.

My heart started pounding,
my knees felt so weak,
But, being a brave kid,
I just HAD to peek.

I pulled back the curtains. My mouth opened wide.
An army of monsters had gathered outside!
They staggered and stumbled and lurched down the streets
With bags full of cookies and candy corn treats.

Emerging from sewers and houses and stores
Came creatures and critters with ravenous roars.
Then more came along from all over the state.
They filled up the streets at a dizzying rate!

From Athens, Columbus, Atlanta, and Rome,
They gathered together outside of my home

To go trick-or-treating
for one **spooky** night,
And seek out the living,
then give them a **fright**.

The thunder clapped loudly with terrible booms.
The witches dodged lightning and clung to their brooms.
The two-headed doggies tried chasing their tails,
And banshees let loose with their hideous wails.

The vampires hung out
on the street in their gangs,
And grinned, just to show off
their pearly white fangs.

JUST
MARRIED IN
GEORGIA

The mummies moaned loudly and swayed side to side,
While Frankenstein stomped about town with his bride.

An alien race from a faraway sun
Came looking for Roswell, but chose the wrong one.

They soon fell in love with our warm Southern charm,
Completely forgetting they came to do harm.

The swamp monster came out of OKefenoKee.
He **roared** and he **roared**
till his voice went all croaKy.

He felt so embarrassed, he hid out of sight.
(A squeaKy swamp monster just doesn't sound right!)

The creepies were crawly, the crazies were crazed,
The zombies from Johns Creek had eyes that were glazed.
The ogres from Macon were ugly as sin,
With big bulging noses and warts on their chin.

The ghouls danced around but were lacking in soul,
The gargoyles could rock, and the headless could roll!
Although the whole spectacle seemed to spell doom,
I foolishly thought I'd be safe in my room!

But then something happened
that made my heart jump.
From somewhere below me
I heard a big THUMP!

I froze for a moment, as quiet as a mouse.
Yes, I could hear noises from INSIDE THE HOUSE!

I put on my slippers

and pulled on my robe.

I shook like a leaf

but I don't think it showed.

Then, slowly but surely,

I crept down the stairs,

Preparing myself for the
biggest of scares.

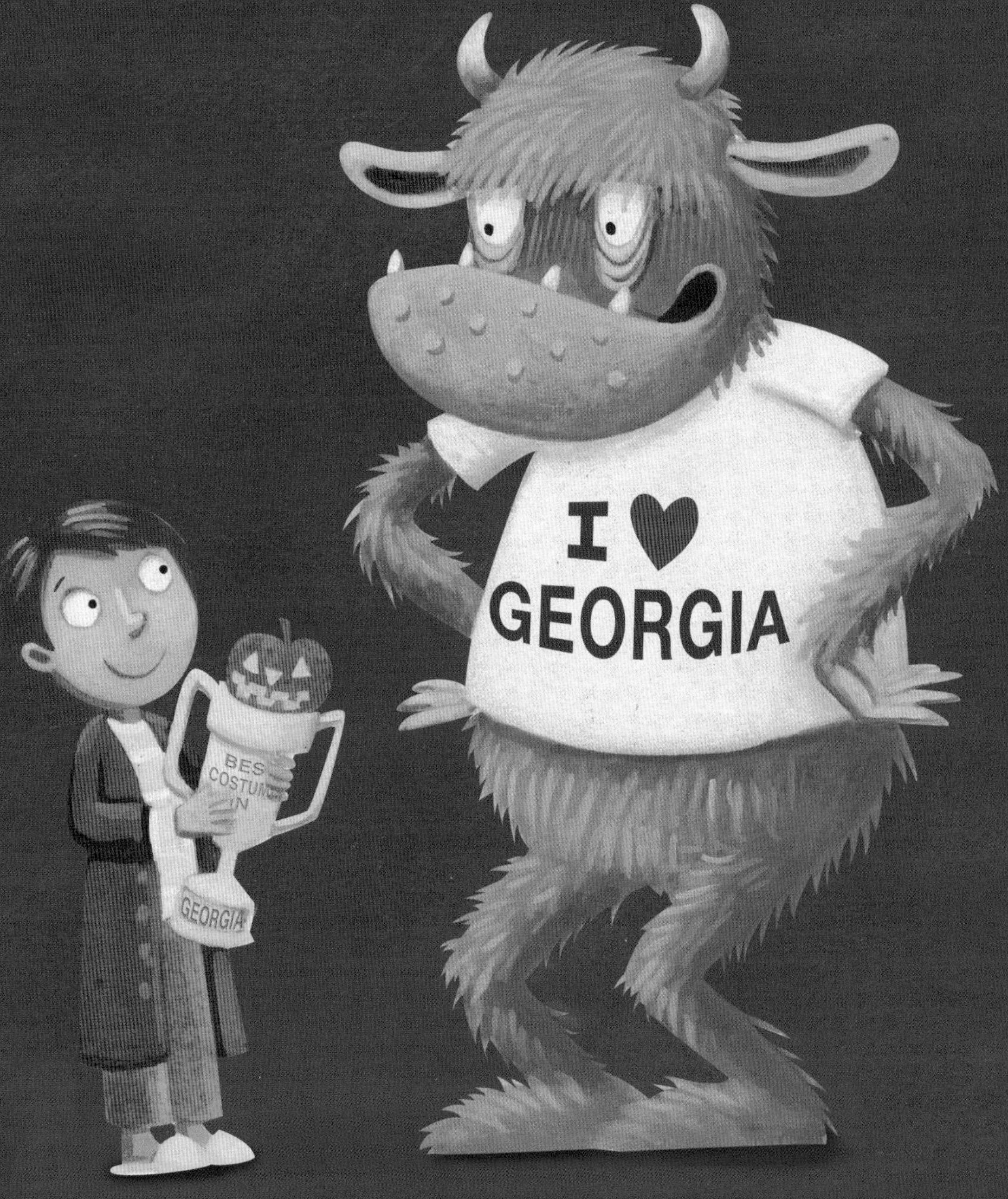
I ♥ GEORGIA
GEORGIA

We partied together
until the moon set,
A Halloween night
that I'll never forget.

And next year I won't
want to hide in my bed.
The monsters won't scare me,